JOSHUA OF GOD

JOSHUA OF GOD

WILLIAM BOFFI

XULON PRESS

Xulon Press
2301 Lucien Way #415
Maitland, FL 32751
407.339.4217
www.xulonpress.com

© 2022 by William Boffi

All rights reserved solely by the author. The author guarantees all contents are original and do not infringe upon the legal rights of any other person or work. No part of this book may be reproduced in any form without the permission of the author.

Due to the changing nature of the Internet, if there are any web addresses, links, or URLs included in this manuscript, these may have been altered and may no longer be accessible. The views and opinions shared in this book belong solely to the author and do not necessarily reflect those of the publisher. The publisher therefore disclaims responsibility for the views or opinions expressed within the work.

Paperback ISBN-13: 978-1-66286-452-0
Ebook ISBN-13: 978-1-66286-453-7

TABLE OF CONTENTS

PART 1:
THE CLONING 1

Chapter 1 3
Chapter 2 9
Chapter 3 19
Chapter 4 23
Chapter 5 29
Chapter 6 31
Chapter 7 35
Chapter 8 37
Chapter 9 49
Chapter 10 51
Chapter 11 53
Chapter 12 55

PART 2:
WHO DO YOU THINK I AM? 57

Chapter 13 59
Chapter 14 63
Chapter 15 65
Chapter 16 69
Chapter 17 71
Chapter 18 75
Chapter 19 79
Chapter 20 83
Chapter 21 59
Chapter 22 89

PART 1
THE CLONING

CHAPTER 1

May 12, 2026
Gloucester, Massachusetts 7:50 a.m.

Little did Bill Benson realize how different his life would become. His laboratory was in Cambridge, adjacent to Harvard University. He was educated at a small Catholic college in Rhode Island, Providence College, founded and staffed by the Dominicans, an Order of Preachers. He majored in mathematics and had an active extracurricular schedule. He was a golfer, played intramural basketball, was a member of the Friars Club, and he volunteered to teach in the confirmation program at a nearby Catholic church. He got his PhD from the Yale Archaeology and Theology programs. He peppered his studies with information technology training at a job he got upon his graduation from Providence College with Blue Cross of Connecticut in New Haven. He had a mother in New Haven, his father died in 2021 and he had no brothers or sisters.

He lived in Gloucester Massachusetts. He loved fishing and was totally dedicated to his research. If he wasn't at his lab, he most likely was out on his New Bedford whaler. He loved mingling with other fishermen.

"Hey Doc, gonna go out today?"

"I can't. Got a meeting today at noon with some people from Italy."

"Italy? Where in Italy are they from? I still have relatives there."

"They're from the Vatican."

"Doc, I got the idea you stay arm's length away from the Church."

"Ben, you're right, and I make no excuses about it, but this has to do with research I am doing that involves some Church cooperation."

So, Bill Benson, PhD, put his briefcase on the passenger seat of his '69 Camaro, his pride and joy. His trip was thirty-nine miles and would take about fifty minutes.

The Isaac Stark Memorial Laboratory was buzzing with an excitement usually associated with innovation and invention. The lab was established through an endowment from a successful Harvard grad, Isaac Stark, who wished to extend genetics research to safely develop the cloning of a human.

The Stark Memorial lab had a set of operating principles to guide its research and a group of CEOs and PhDs from key areas of expertise and disciplines: global corporate leaders, theologians, psychologists, clergy, lawyers, and politicos from all over the globe to help in critical decision-making as a project progressed.

THE STARK MEMORIAL LABORATORY ADVISORY BOARD

Chairperson Louise Palmieri – CIO and corporate futurist, Intel

Larry Harmon – CEO, Bank of America

J Dan Rafferty – president, Notre Dame University

CHAPTER 1

Jeanine Boisvert – chairman of psychology department, Massachusetts General Hospital

Cardinal Giuseppe Gandolfo – dean of Vatican Theological School

James Sheridan, OP – Bishop of Cincinnati, Ohio

Carmen Oliver – editor-in-chief, USA Today

James Toms – corporate attorney to several biotech corporations

"Good morning, Cindy. Have our guests arrived yet?"

"No, Dr. Benson. They are arriving at Logan at 10:05 a.m. They should be here by noon."

"That's good. It gives me a chance to meet with the Pope." He placed a kiss on Cindy's head.

They met at a job fair in Providence. Professor Benson had just landed the position of chief executive officer at Stark Laboratory, with a grant to establish a research company to study innovation in the global scientific community. He was looking for an administrative assistant on whom he could depend on in tough situations. After speaking with a dozen or so applicants, Cindy was sitting at the applicant's seat and Bill looked up. He knew immediately that she was the one. She would go onto answer Bill's queries with grace and confidence. The next day, he called her and made an offer, which she accepted. They agreed that she would begin her new career on Monday of the next week.

"Do you think we might begin our new careers over dinner this Saturday?" asked Bill.

Cindy responded, "My mind says to keep our relationship on a professional level; my heart is telling me that you will be a big part of my life for a long time. My mom taught me, 'When in doubt, follow your heart.' I would love to go to dinner with you."

This interchange was an epiphany that validated the respect and love they both felt. Cindy would be a focal point in Bill's life, more than either of them could imagine. Bill would aspire to lead his company to change the world, a theme that his first major project would embody.

They hugged and left, satisfied with their agreement. They met for dinner on Saturday. The menu was perfect. There was music. They danced, ate and drank, all the time, falling in love. They left the restaurant hand in hand. Bill drove Cindy home and walked her to her front door; when it was time to leave, they kissed. It was a great way to begin their relationship.

He made his way to his office. Cindy followed him in with a mug of coffee and the agenda for that day's meeting. She turned and left, closing the door behind her. Bill and Cindy dated for a while but decided to go slowly with building an intimate relationship so they could build the Isaac Stark Laboratory, a business whose primary focus is on cloning—human cloning.

Bill Benson needed the next hour and a half to ensure that his presentation was on point. *How will I solve moral and ethical issues surrounding this highly controversial project? What if we don't get it right the first time? What do we do with the biological and testing waste that we know will result? What are the implications this work will cause for non-scientific disciplines? How will the Church react to this proposal?* He had visited Vatican City over the first three months of 2025. To his surprise, Pope Paul was receptive to the concept of using the Shroud of Turin to clone the person whose blood was on the Shroud. He became

CHAPTER 1

a willing ally to Bill Benson. They both visited sites renowned for cloning. Doors to top-secret labs flew open to the Pope. Pope Paul and Bill Benson were developing a knowledge base of cloning to help in determining the best practices in human cloning. They needed to be experts in this field to bring it into a church synod. The plan that was unfolding required that the Pope and Dr. Benson represented cloning as a twenty-first-century reality acceptable to the modern Church.

The challenge was enormous; their plan was daunting. Their strategy would be to go right at the doubters by representing that the choice of Jesus being cloned from the blood He shed on the Shroud was, in fact, a matter of faith. After all, He promised to come again. But could it be that simple? Did He *leave* blood stains as the catalyst to return Him to His humanity, and if so, what would be the impact on the Church?

In 2025, cloning mammals was developed like any other agricultural technique to improve quality in the products farmers produce. It required regulations and monitoring, to ensure the local and global environment is preserved.

In the late twentieth century, cloning of mammals had limited success, despite the successful cloning of a lamb named Dolly on July 5, 1996. The procedure involved the harvesting of the donor's DNA from skin cells, the process of sending an electric pulse through the donor's egg, and a surrogate lamb who supplied an egg with the DNA removed to be fused with the donor's egg and then implanted in the surrogate.

CHAPTER 2

May 12, 2026
Agenda for meeting with Pope Paul VII

Attendees:
Bill Benson – CEO, chief of science and technology, Stark Labs.

Visitors:
Pope Paul VII

Cardinal Gandolfo – dean, Vatican Theological School

Louise Palmieri – chairwoman, Stark Advisory Board

Alonzo Gonsalves, PhD, JD – technology and science advisor to Pope Paul VII

Davide Bartolomeo – corporate lawyer and life sciences technology consultant to Pope Paul VII

AGENDA

1. Welcome to Stark Lab – Dr. Benson
2. Purpose of the meeting – Dr. Benson
3. Vatican reaction

4. Q&A
5. Lunch

Over the last several decades, the scientific community had developed new methods, political insight, and scientific guidelines for cloning mammals, and in 1996, Dolly the Sheep became the first successfully cloned mammal. Over the course of the twenty-first century, many more instances of mammal cloning were introduced. The idea of cloning mammals has been driven by biological duplication to ensure the survival of the planet and the improvement of the quality of life.

The project on the drawing board at Stark Lab to be discussed that day was the cloning of a specific human being who lived His life in a way that motivated many generations of humans. In fact, He presumably died to save humanity, and it is believed by many that Jesus Christ was resurrected from the dead.

While Christians have certainty, through their faith, that He is the Son of God, we know very little about the man, His origin, and His history. Benson will present to the Vatican visitors a proposal to clone the person whose blood is on the Shroud. In so doing, he hoped to expose the human nature and history of Jesus.

Over the past five years, the Church had survived some thorny issues troubling the last two Popes. The Pope in 2025 was Pope Paul (VII). The last eight Popes from 1958 were:

1. Pope Paul VII — current Pope (late2024-)
2. Pope Alexander IX — May 2022–2024
3. Pope Francis — March 13, 2013–April 2022
4. Benedict XVI — April 19, 2005–Feb. 28, 2013

CHAPTER 2

5. John Paul II — Oct. 16, 1978–April 2, 2005
6. John Paul I — Aug. 26–Sept. 28, 1978
7. Paul VI — June 21, 1963–Aug. 6, 1978
8. John XXIII — Oct. 28, 1958–June 3, 1963

The years leading up to Pope Paul's ascension were a roller-coaster ride for him. He was a widowed man in the service of the of the U.N. He served in the capacity of an intelligence officer and was promoted to chief of negotiations during peace talks involving the U.N. and major Middle East countries. He became renowned as the peacemaker. His efforts during the difficult time in his life did not go unnoticed. This remarkable accomplishment was noticed by Pope Alexander. He contacted Antonio and asked him to come to the Vatican.

Pope Alexander shared a plan he had developed to bring him into Vatican life. He needed a surrogate to exercise papal authority in the complex process of solving the stain of cover-up that the Church was dealing with. He was well into a solution but did not have the real solution unless he could bring in a person who possessed the skills, understanding, and courage to bring this scourge to an end. He was convinced Antonio Indeglia possessed these qualities.

He convened a clandestine quorum of cardinals and told them his dilemma and his preferences. He explained that Antonio Indeglia must be lifted to the office of cardinal. They reflected for several days and presented to Pope Alexander a plan to adopt Antonio. It called for an accelerated preparation for the priesthood. An ordination by the Pope, this would ease his ascension to cardinal. Once he became a priest, the Pope's job of making him a cardinal was a matter of following the rules and canon law associated with appointing a cardinal.

He accepted the plan and contacted Antonio. As they began their discussions, there was hesitation by Antonio, which was ameliorated by the Pope's exuberance and commitment. He was drawn to believing that the plan was possible. After much discussion and many sleepless nights, they agreed to move forward. Antonio began studying for the priesthood. His mentors were the men that the Pope brought in from all over and with many disciplines. He impressed each of his tutors with his wisdom and faith. In the end, he was ordained into the priesthood. He embraced his new life with passion and a real desire to serve God and the Pope. He was exposed to the severity of the Church's pedophilia scandal and began to think about the scandal and its solution as a negotiation.

He met with as many of the cast of characters in this scandal as he was allowed to. Slowly but surely, he began to understand what the solution entailed:

- A complete admission by the Pope that the coverup had happened and many souls were involved.
- A willingness by the Pope to dedicate his papacy to bring this scourge to its knees, to abolish any obstacles to the solution.
- A promise to put in place "firewalls" and other processes to identify and eliminate the possibility of scandals like this one being repeated.

It was clear what the solution was, and Antonio was ready to take on this mission. It took months to iron out his ascension to cardinal. The Pope worked diligently to ensure enough support for Antonio. His vision was gaining strength among the cardinals. There was an easier way to gain Antonio's cardinalship.

CHAPTER 2

That was through papal mandate. But the Pope would then be put in the position of defending his choice, an action obviously reminiscent of the old Church. He never wavered and stayed the course, but his persistence was wearing on him and his health began to fail. That was his reward for his persistence.

The day came when the subject of Father Indeglia was brought to the curia. Should he be promoted to cardinal based on his ability to mitigate the scandal? The discussions were filled with passion and Church loyalty. How will this appointment support the Church's mission?

At the end of a month of debate, the Pope called for a vote. The result was 2/3 of the cardinals supported the Pope in installing Father Indeglia as a cardinal. This was an overwhelming attestation of the Pope's credibility among the faithful. The day after the red skullcap was placed on his head, Father Indeglia began to implement the papal direction to resolve the issue plaguing the Church.

In six months, he brought the parties and their counsels to the table with Church counsel. It would take months to iron out "who owes what to whom." There were many attempts to undermine the Church's new direction on the coverup, most of which came from uninformed groups inside the Church. This was a disappointment to Cardinal Indeglia and the Pope, but it had to be resolved before they could move on.

Eventually, this obstacle was overcome with a monetary settlement of $900 million, which served to raise a caution flag to Church officials to be vigilant concerning internal scandals. Meanwhile, Pope Alexander became increasingly ill and feeble. Once the work of negotiating a settlement was completed, the Pope turned fatally ill and died.

The next major task was to select a new Pope to carry on Pope Alexander's legacy. Antonio Indeglia was the frontrunner going into the election. It only took one round of voting before the white smoke flew from the Vatican chimney. The announcement and the new Pope's introduction to the world happened when he appeared on the balcony and was greeted with cheers of "paciere." This, the Italian word for "peacemaker."

THIS BEGAN THE PAPACY OF POPE PAUL VII

As soon as he was elected Pope Paul VII, he changed the age-old paradigm of women's role in the Church. In 2026, women were finally welcomed into the priesthood.

This and several other significant changes led to a Renaissance at the Vatican. In the past, there was an automatic assumption of "no" to newness and innovation. Technology was the enemy of the Church. Pope Paul VII changed that. He is open to newness and found himself at a point in history when change was not only accepted, but also welcomed. What the Church needed at this point in its evolution was a way of showing the world it was ready to change the planet.

So, the guests today were being led by Pope Paul VII. He brought with him two Vatican lawyers. Dr. Benson hosted the meeting, and he invited two members of his advisory panel to attend and assist in the formal request to take some samples from the blood stains on the Shroud. He would explain the science behind cloning, the history of successful cloning, and the possible impact on the faithful of the results of cloning the blood on the Shroud. Rather than portraying a trouble-free project, he would emphasize the problems that would arise as progress was made, emphasizing the need to control mistakes. His advisory board had recommended a single attempt at the entire process.

CHAPTER 2

This would limit the problem associated with cloning waste to a single attempt, thus limiting the amount of activity associated with destroying the byproducts of The Cloning.

They discussed the history of the Shroud and emphasized the need for limited handling and delicacy when touching the Shroud.

The Sacred Shroud was also known as the Shroud of Turin because it was kept in Torino, Italy and protected from outside influences. It is displayed under glass in front of the Cathedral of John the Baptist in the heart of Turin. The Shroud, like all relics in the Church, had a story.

When Jesus gave himself up, He was treated like a criminal. He was whipped and beaten and mocked. The Romans were experts in torture and imposing death on their criminals and enemies. Before He was crucified, which is how He would eventually die, He was scourged, and a crown of thorns was jammed into His skull, causing blood to stream down His face. Then, He was forced to carry the cross. When they arrived at the crucifixion site, He was nailed to the cross. Most depictions of the crucified Christ depict Him nailed through his palms and feet, which would not hold the body very long on the cross. He was nailed just below the wrist. Jesus died on the cross in front of His loved ones. He was removed from the cross, anointed, and blessed before the sabbath. As is the custom, He was wrapped in clean linen burial cloth and placed in a tomb that was sealed at its entrance. His friends and followers dispersed. This was on the Friday before Easter Sunday.

Then, on a bright, glorious First Easter Sunday, two women went to the tomb to check that all was right. What they found was the beginning of a revolution in the world. The stone in front of the entrance was rolled aside, and inside the tomb, they found the Shroud, but Jesus was gone. They took the Shroud and went to tell the others what they found. Believers know through faith that Jesus was resurrected, rose from the dead, and showed His risen body to His disciples.

The Shroud bore information His followers would not necessarily have noticed in the tomb, but they knew they had the burial cloth of Jesus. The Shroud was moved out of the Holy Land during the Crusades. The earliest historical records of the Shroud of Turin place it in Lirey, France during the 1350s. Later, it suffered burns in a fire. After that, people started noticing the burn marks on the Shroud. In time, the Shroud was passed to whomever had enough money to buy it. At one point in its travels, people noticed what looked like a photographic negative. Upon further investigation, the blood marks were where they should be, at the wrists, at the ankles, and at the forehead. Believers would say the photo marks were there to record the moment at which He rose from the dead, a sort of flash photo of the resurrection. Non-believers would say they were painted on the Shroud, but this turned out to be wrong. The marks have not yielded an agreed-upon solution, even with modern digital imaging technology. The bottom line at this point is that, scientifically, no one knows how the marks got there.

Dr. Benson stated that the purpose of The Cloning project would be to identify to the world the person whose blood was there. He was certain he could clone the person whose blood was on the Shroud. However, he needed to observe the cloned human to identify God in Jesus. A conclusion identifying the Shroud's hidden persona as anyone other than Jesus would mean that a public relations campaign would need to be developed explaining that the Shroud's authenticity was not a faith mandate, whether it was authentic or not. The faithful know

CHAPTER 2

through faith and sacred scripture that Jesus is God and that He was resurrected from the dead. A finding that the Shroud contained Jesus' blood was simply an attestation of what the faithful already know.

But how does cloning Jesus change the world? Hasn't He come once and caused the world to believe? Isn't that what the faithful believe?

The Pope and Dr. Benson discussed this at length, both today and on numerous other occasions during 2025. They agreed that the motivation to clone Jesus lies in Jesus' original mission—evangelization, proselytization, and education of non-believers. His cloning would begin His second coming. Dr. Benson and Pope Paul VII were convinced that Jesus left His blood on the Shroud because He knew that one day, science would assist in His return.

Pope Paul's assistance was wonderful. He told the committee about a project already underway to analyze the blood and carbon date it. The Vatican had already approved this project, so it looked like adding the cloning of the blood to this effort was a great fit. The results and forensic evidence gained in that project were stored in the Vatican archives. Only the Pope had access and clearance to the archives.

The Pope stated emphatically that he approved moving forward; he pointed out that he would like to take the proposal back to the Vatican, where he would convene a holy conclave to wrestle with this proposal and submit their collective opinion back to him. He stated that the new renaissance in the Holy Mother Church would help move the project along with minimum delays. Also, what he left unstated was that he wanted to flush out those cardinals that were hardliners in the previous regime. Dr. Benson knew the Pope well; he was sure of his commitment. The Pope didn't know the extent to which the College of Cardinals will agree with him, nor did he know the number of cardinals who would be backing down. He needed to address this upon his return to the Vatican. As most entrepreneurs know, you must have buy-in from your constituents, in this case, the College of Cardinals.

The meeting ended at 2:30 p.m. Pope Paul returned to the Vatican with his two companions.

CHAPTER 3

May 15, 2026
Vatican City

It didn't take long for the news of a "secret" meeting in the United States, which the Pope attended, to circulate around the smallest country in the world, The Vatican. The rumors reached the College of Cardinals.

According to the Pope's early intelligence, three cardinals from the old guard began to meet to build a plan to sabotage the project devised in Cambridge before they even knew what the plan was.

After the meeting in Cambridge, the Pope and Bill Benson were energized by the discussion and the decision to move forward with The Cloning. In his excitement, the Pope made several phone calls to confidantes at the Vatican, not realizing how fast word of such a bold direction would travel. As iron filings crowd around a magnet, the sensational news of a cloning drew in both supporters and dissenters.

It would seem logical that those in the support category would realize that acting quickly and not waiting for the Pope to make a formal announcement of his intention of cloning from bloodstains on the Shroud would cause problems but their exuberance overwhelmed their reasoning. Some of his supporters in the curia began to plan for The Cloning. This proved to be a major error in collective judgment. The Pope, on his arrival from Cambridge, was greeted with supposition and erroneous assumptions. The Pope came under fire by news agencies and local news purveyors. He obviously did not expect this. The usual media were supplanted by large media giants looking for the exclusive scoop. Now, most of the cardinals had their own media ties. When asked, they could only rely on conjecture, which was portrayed by the media as fact. This misunderstanding by well-meaning clergy was what Pope supporters caused.

On the dissenter side, there was opposition; the most vocal were the three cardinals who wanted the Pope identified as a heretic. They had ties to ancient societies that had haunted the papacy for centuries. The most important one related to the Shroud, the Sancta Sindone, was committed to protecting the Shroud at all costs. Word of The Cloning caused this band of bullies to mobilize and begin planning for the discrediting of the perpetrators of such an outcry, fueled by the three cardinals who were the nemesis of the Pope. Violence erupted in all of Italy.

The level of outcry was not limited to the Vatican. This sensational news story was felt around the world. Even before the Pope had a chance to begin planning for the global announcement, there was a demand for accommodations in and around Rome. As people from around the globe began to arrive, there were incidents of violence, as many people were denied accommodations due to overbooking.

Outside Rome, in the rest of Italy, rioters were prodded to commit acts of violence. Rioters were active in every major metropolitan area in Italy, and police departments were overwhelmed. Italy was in the grips of anarchy. Gangs of thugs were

CHAPTER 3

called in to increase the pressure on all the municipalities In Italy. Sacra Sindone was at the core of this uprising and would continue in this role until the Pope could take corrective action.

This was not a good start to the Pope's plan to clone the blood from the Sacred Shroud. He needed to talk to Bill Benson.

The Pope had their phones tapped and their computers placed on separate servers months ago. All incoming and outgoing communications would be logged and saved for later review. A private security firm had been hired to track their movements and record suspicious activity.

The papal phone system became deadlocked, and the phone company was trying to determine the reason for the chaos; it all seemed to boil down to the Cambridge meeting the day before. It seemed that the Pope may have misread the magnitude of "other" issues that might arise due to rumors.

Around the world, there were self-serving reactions from world leaders. For instance, In Tel-Aviv, there was concern based on early feedback, that the papal meeting in Cambridge might somehow put Israel in a position of weakness. Benjamin Netanyahu placed a call to the Pope. The Pope's secretary took a message to have the Pope return Mr. Netanyahu's call. The message never got to the Pope. The Church was in a state of confusion, and it was an embarrassment.

In another instance with the phone system deadlocked, the National Security Agency (NSA) received an alert that something was going on at the Vatican that was a potential security breach for the USA. They contacted the Vatican police to find out what was going on. That message was lost in the chaos of the phone system traffic jam. The message never got to anyone.

Pope Paul returned to his suite in the Vatican. He had reports in front of him about the "crisis" the previous day. There was no evidence from any of his sources of widespread conspiracies. His plan was to hold a papal synod within the next three months to address the Cambridge meeting with the rest of the world.

And so, the call went out to all the cardinals all over the world and to bishops and archbishops and all those faithful who felt strongly about church matters that the Pope had called for a synod to address the truth about the Shroud of Turin and its importance in the Church of the future. The correspondence included the history of the Shroud and its importance in today's Church. Also included was a reference to cloning the blood left on the Shroud. The communication explained that the result of The Cloning may produce a copy of the crucified man whose image is on the Shroud. The ecclesiastical and theological implications need to be vetted and debated, as was done in early church councils when the nature of Jesus was debated. This became the focus of the synod. The communications included a description of cloning in easily understood language. Also, there was a primer on church councils. The list of invitees contained 220 cardinals; and the remaining invitations would go to 140 prominent bishops and forty archbishops from around the world and about 100ordinary Catholic people, the leading Catholic thinkers from the global laity. Any less would cause a feeling of exclusion. Any more would result in a lack of control at the synod.

There was widespread acceptance about the need for this church council. The Pope had set the synod to begin on June 22, 2026. An all-out effort was begun. Plans for lodging, internet access, feeding the 500, and numerous logistical issues were arranged. The Vatican would host the most important synod in centuries. Pope Paul VII was delighted.

CHAPTER 4

The Uprising
Late May 2026

It wasn't native Italians who caused the initial confusion and consternation in Rome and at the Vatican.

Thousands of curious visitors from all over the world descended on the hotels, motels, boarding houses, and campgrounds. All available marina slots were commandeered as potential alternate living quarters. Hordes of visitors descended on Rome. Traffic was horrendous. Restaurant reservations were impossible to get.

The triumvirate found out about the synod and what would be asked of the Church. They seized the opportunity to sabotage the Pope's project to clone Jesus. Each of the triumvirate cardinals had ties to notorious people who would do almost anything to leverage their influence inside the Church hierarchy. So, when the confusion began, they called in the Sacra Sindone. The triumvirate had ties to the Sacra Sindone, having "assisted" them in, among other nefarious deeds, the invalidating of carbon dating the Shroud data on several attempts.

The level of violence rose very quickly in Rome and the Vatican as a result of this intervention. Tourists and travelers were assaulted, beaten, and robbed. There was a rash of sexual assaults and kidnappings of women and children, whom people were saying might have been sold into slavery. The Roman Carabinieri were overwhelmed, as was the Vatican Police and the Pope's protectors, the Swiss Guard.

The violence began to move into other cities in southern Italy and Sicily. The country's law enforcement officials were frustrated and didn't know where to turn. They formed a union and decided to petition the Pope.

Pope Paul VII opened the missive from the law enforcement community in Italy. It read:

Your Holiness, Pope Paul VII,

We, the officials charged with enforcing the laws of Italy, are running out of resources to keep the peace in the major cities in our ancient and beautiful country. The streets are battlegrounds, and the blood of our countrymen is being spilled every day as well as the blood of tourists and visitors.

We need your help to battle this violence. We'd like to send a cadre of three of our leading officials to meet with you. Our mission is to reach a truce with the perpetrators of this violence.

I await your reply, and once I hear from you, I will contact your secretary to coordinate this meeting.

Sincerely,

It was signed by Dante Folingiere, police chief, Naples, Italy.

CHAPTER 4

Pope Paul VII reacted quickly. He instructed his secretary to contact Chief Folingiere and set the meeting time and date. He then reached for the phone to contact Bill Benson to let him know what was happening. The phone rang four times before Bill answered.

"Pope Paul, how can I help you?" His greeting short and to the point.

Pope Paul VII related all that he knew about the violence and the grave predicament he found himself in. When he finished, there was a long pause.

Then Professor Benson replied: "Your Excellency, I'm afraid there is no choice for either of us. For your part, you need to remain in charge. You need to cancel the synod and let me take it from here. I will need access to the Shroud at some point. I heard the same feedback from my investigators. They advised me to disappear. They said there is a bounty on my head of $250,000. I need to go underground. I'll contact you in a little while. Good luck, Your Holiness."

"Bill, I want you to know that I am committed to the project, and I will support it to the best of my ability. Do what you need to do to get the project back on track, and I'll support you from here."

"Your Holiness, I have some information about the rioting and the violence sweeping the country. I have learned that the triumvirate has brought in a little-known society that is sworn to protect the Shroud of Turin, no matter the risk to its members or the extent of violence it may cause. You should meet with the Folingiere group and let them know of this heinous alliance. When discussion leads to, "What can you do for us, Pope Paul," you can spring a plan designed to end the violence. You can suggest that you and the Folingiere group contact Sacra

Sindone, set up a peace conference, and let them know that Sacra Sindone will become a part of the Vatican Police, and they will be forgiven their past offenses, and their raison d'etre will be forever protected by the Pope if the senseless violence stops immediately. You know how to handle this negotiation. It's not unlike your performance in the Middle East peace initiative. Your promises will carry the discussion to the right conclusion; we need to stop the violence. I need to go now. I must speak with Cindy to get things started."

The society of Sacra Sindone was first established by a papal mandate in the fourteenth century; its purpose was to protect the Shroud from outside influences. It was brought to the Pope's attention that this sacred relic had quite a provenance. This history came as result of Church records and evidence found on the Shroud. The case that was brought forward by several cardinals was very compelling, resulting in the papal mandate. The mandate contained the Society's purpose and structure. The Society would answer to the Pope and would be governed through the College of Cardinals. The mandate called for two cardinals to be elected by the College of Cardinals to be the Society's leaders. They had the latitude to alter the governance and purpose of the Society. There was no provision for papal oversight.

Thus, the Society set its own direction and rules for the next six centuries. In those intervening years, the Shroud was enshrined at the cathedral in Torino, Italy. As a result of twentieth-century technological advances, the markings and stains on the Shroud came under scrutiny. As more and more interest in the Shroud increased, the Society became a police force.

At the time, the leadership of the Sacra Sindone increased the Society's membership to include a network of believers around the globe. They established links to important people

CHAPTER 4

in the political and criminal world. They were able to mobilize their resources in a very short time to "protect the Shroud."

Word of the possibility of harvesting DNA from bloodstains on the Shroud came to the attention of the two cardinals in charge of Sacra Sindone. The membership was put on high alert. During the twentieth century, interest in the Shroud had resulted in a search for "thugs" to incite and intimidate scientists, theologians, and politicians to stave off any access to the Shroud by any means necessary.

As soon as the meeting in Cambridge ended, the Pope called his administrative assistant and told him what had transpired. He especially stressed that the decision was made to move forward with The Cloning. This call was recorded by the Sacra Sindone. The two cardinals immediately set in motion the orders to riot.

The call ended, and they both hung up, not knowing whether they'd see each other again. The Pope went back to planning his meeting with law enforcement in Italy, and Dr. Benson dialed his office number at Stark Laboratories. Cindy picked up on the second ring.

As soon as he hung up, the Pope instructed his assistant and confidante to contact Chief Folingiere to arrange a meeting with the group of law enforcement officials he represents. Reverend Carlo Pennicchini contacted Chief Folingiere and scheduled the meeting for three law enforcement people and the Pope. That meeting was scheduled for 10:00 a.m. on Friday, June 20, 2026.

The Pope remained committed to the project, but he had to remain in control of the Church while beset by the triumvirate. He had to maintain his position of strength and he had to call off the synod because of the violence. He had to disassociate from The Cloning. He convinced the triumvirate to stop the violence by exonerating them. They agreed to stop the violence if the Pope did not support Benson in his quest to clone Jesus. The Pope met with the law enforcement group and informed them that he had put measures in place to stop the violence. However, he went on to say that the triumvirate were exonerated, and Sacra Sindone would not be brought to justice because their passion for the Shroud would help protect it beyond The Cloning.

The Pope demanded that the triumvirate cease undermining papal authority and asked them to remain distant from each other. Their rank as cardinals was on the line.

CHAPTER 5

2026
Cambridge Massachusetts,

"Stark Laboratories, Cindy speaking."
"Hi Cindy, it's Bill."
"Bill, what's going on?"
"Young lady, if I told you, I'd have to kill you!"
"Oh, I'm so sorry."
"Just kidding, but I am going to ask you to help me out of a tough situation."
"You know I'll do whatever you need. Let me get a steno pad to take some notes." Bill Benson filled Cindy in on all he needed.

1. He needed her to find him lodging in Rome under a different identity.
2. He needed her to lease space through another person. Enough space to build a cloning lab. He told her who to work with at Stark to design the lab.
3. He needed her to move some scientists to Italy, separately, and have them report to the new lab in Italy in a matter of three weeks. He would let her know when and who.

4. He needed her to make all the travel arrangements including passports, driver's licenses, plane reservations, hotel arrangements.
5. He assured her that he would be there for her at every step.

"And by the way, I'm going to need you here for a very special assignment. You'll get a raise in pay and a place to live. You'll be committed for five to seven years, and you'll need to take care of an infant for the first three years. I know I'm asking a lot, so I'd understand if you say no."

"I was wondering how you were going to raise a child after The Cloning. I love you, and I accept the challenge and agree to all your requirements. Thanks, Dr. Benson. I love you, Bill."

CHAPTER 6

Joshua's Early Life
Spring 2027

The tasks given to Cindy Gibbons began immediately because the assignment given to Cindy left little time to spare.

Cindy enthusiastically took on the assignment to relocate employees of the Stark Institute to Italy to support The Cloning. She needed little direction since she knew every person and their accomplishments at the Institute. Dr. Benson knew this and that was why he chose her to spearhead the move.

Cindy found a place for Benson to live. It was in the Roman countryside, just south of Rome.

Her next task was to list the things to be accomplished leading to The Cloning. The institute employed scientists and IT professionals. The process went smoothly. She listed all the employees and their areas of expertise. She then interviewed each. Many of them had made their lives in Massachusetts and had real problems pulling up stakes to live and work in Italy. She identified fifteen of them to be relocated.

Next, she began the search for available space in and around Latina to house the Italian branch of the Stark Institute. Her search resulted in several available sites. She looked at each and narrowed the sites down to two locations, Arce and Latina.

Her next step was to find places for the displaced employees to live. The search was limited to sites within a fifteen-minute commute from either of the potential laboratory sites. She chose Arce for the site of the laboratory.

The process was interrupted by a period of violence aimed at the fifteen employees chosen to relocate. It seems that Sacra Sindone got their hands on a partial list of the employees chosen to move to Italy. The thugs had no idea what the list entailed. The employees were accosted by the Society and interrogated. When three of them attempted to flee their captors, they were found and killed.

Luckily, the information Sacra Sindone had intercepted was all they had. The moves were completed before Sacra Sindone could recover any more information. Cindy built a series of manual and digital firewalls that served to protect her move data. It proved very effective.

She found a house in nearby Latina for Dr. Benson. She chose it with the knowledge that she and Bill Benson would live there and raise the cloned infant together.

She then selected a residence for each employee. Once this was completed, she began moving the employees to their new homes. At the same time, she began furnishing the laboratory space she had chosen as the Italian branch of Stark Laboratory.

The laboratory space was a relatively new warehouse located in Arce, Italy, a beautiful Italian center of science and technology.

Cindy and Professor Benson later moved to their house in Latina to accept and raise the newborn infant from The Cloning.

Cindy aimed to complete all these tasks prior to The Cloning. The laboratory was completed early in March 2027. The moves were completed by March 15, 2027.

CHAPTER 6

JANUARY 5, 2028

Benson inspected his new digs. There were five rooms, three bedrooms and two baths—too much space for a single person, but he was comfortable there. He called the local cable company and had cable installed. Then he moved in.

On the night before The Cloning, Bill Benson opened the door to Cindy's room. He walked to the couch on which she was seated. He held her hand and spoke in a low tone.

"Cindy, I love you, and I'm praying that all goes well tomorrow. You alone are the right person for The Cloning."

"Let's talk about you and me tomorrow."

JANUARY 6, 2028

The blood from the Shroud was cloned; The procedure was new but had been tested extensively.

At the proper time, the embryo was implanted into Cindy's womb. Something unexplained happened during The Cloning: a rumble, as of thunder, and the noise of wind swept through the. The cloned embryo started to divide, mimicking a natural birth. Cindy seemed unharmed by the process. The Cloning was a success on the first try.

Benson and Cindy gave him a name: Joshua (YAHWEH is salvation).

Once The Cloning was done, Benson and Cindy began their lives as parents of Joshua. They needed to establish the baby Joshua in an environment that would lead to a normal boyhood.

Sacra Sindone found out that the Shroud had been used for cloning. They claimed the Pope went back on his word so, they began a vendetta against Joshua and Benson, promising to find them and take them out.

CHAPTER 7

Joshua's Early Life
2028-2041

Joshua was born on September 9, 2028. Not unexpectedly, Bill Benson and Cindy Gibbons married in the spring of 2028. They became the parents of Joshua. They were very happy.

Joshua's infancy was spent in Latina, Italy, close to where Joshua was born. Professor Benson was an entrepreneur and business consultant in Rome. Cindy was a stay-at-home mom. She took Joshua out for walks every day where he could interact with other children.

Upon reaching two years old, Joshua was speaking English and Italian with his. parents. He was remarkably affable with his friends and their parents. People enjoyed talking to him. He rarely cried, but when he did, it was when he sensed danger. As he grew, he became a scholastic, religious, and ethical advisor to his friends, teachers, and whoever approached him for help. Bill Benson made a note of all of Joshua's extraordinary actions. Cindy's love for Joshua grew every day.

In one encounter, a group of teenagers surrounded him and began taunting him. He went up to the leader, placed his hands on the youth's head and spoke in an unknown language. The youth dropped to his knees. He looked at Joshua and whispered to him, "Thank you. I didn't know what to do; it felt like I was being swept away."

"Please be careful, Joshua," Cindy whispered.

All the while, Sacra Sindone had spies who were also taking note of this extraordinary young man. They knew of all his good deeds. They knew this was Joshua, the person cloned from the blood from the Shroud of Jesus. They also knew the date of The Cloning.

Cindy and Bill talked about all Joshua's actions knowing that, in time, Joshua would bring about controversy and a demand to know who he was. One night, while they were discussing Joshua's impact on people, the thought was that they should consider relocating. They discussed where they should go. They decided that they should return to their country of origin, the USA. The next day, they began planning to move back to Boston. Joshua was turning thirteen; he was scheduled to attend Dorchester High School. They would live in Brookline.

And so, they moved to Brookline in Boston to begin Joshua's next phase in his life. It was in the spring of 2041. Brookline was a perfect place for Joshua to be in his teenage years.

CHAPTER 8

*Spring 4041-
Joshua's Middle Years*

In Boston, Cindy found employment as a tour guide at the Kennedy Library. Her history degree made her an ideal guide. Professor Benson applied for and gained a professorship at Boston College in Brookline.

Joshua fit quite well into his freshman class at Dorchester High. Somewhere toward the end of his freshman year, he realized his identity and his mission. He had a group of four freshmen whom he admired and loved. These individuals became lifelong friends of Joshua. They sought his counsel when there was doubt about what path to take in life. They learned from him. They called Joshua "teacher." They were extremely loyal to Joshua, often discussing world and local issues well into the night. As for Joshua, he was very happy combing the internet for those in need. When he found people that needed his help urgently, he went to them; he spoke to them about their despair and fear of what life held in store for them. Sometimes one or more of the four followers went with him. He saved hundreds of lives from the grip of hopelessness and desperation.

From a distance, Bill Benson wrote everything down about Joshua. It amazed him how much Joshua was devoted to others. He was becoming convinced that Joshua was Jesus, the Son of God.

As the valedictorian of his Dorchester High School class, Joshua gave a graduation speech that was nothing short of amazing. He beckoned his classmates to serve their brothers and sisters in need. He asked them to live lives of service to others. He stressed that a person does not need to be Mother Theresa or Gandhi to make an impact on the world. Simply serving those in need with a pure heart can make a crease in the universe that will draw others to do the same.

Joshua did not disappoint anyone with his valedictory message. Parents were very receptive to his moving message to their newly graduated offspring. Teachers and administrators basked in the glow that it was due to their excellence that such a human being came to Dorchester. In general, all who met and spoke with Josh were instilled with a special feeling. During his years at Dorchester High School, Joshua honed his people skills. In particular, he had a following of hundreds of people associated with the school and all the support staff who tended the flock.

Joshua held his four closest friends in high esteem. He led them and taught them what it meant to be a good human being. He spent a lot of time cleaning up the misery in their lives. They responded with loyalty and adulation. Their names were Mike Travis, Joe Kershaw, Larry Lukowitz, and Lisa Luongo. They had no plans for their lives beyond having a great summer.

When they were in high school, these five met every day after school in a parking lot three blocks from the school. They each brought a chair and snacks. They sat in a semi-circle and Joshua sat facing them. This time was no different.

CHAPTER 8

Joshua appeared preoccupied as he began to speak.

"You four people mean the world to me. That's what I wanted to discuss today. I have been growing in all phases of life, and you are a part of that. I now fully understand what my mission on this earth is. And I need you to be my ambassadors to the world. You will deal with leaders in the areas of random violence, gun violence, and poverty.

"There are people who know about the incidents of violent crimes. These experts know what the problems are and have real solutions. The world needs to solve these problems. I need the four of you to bring the latest information into the light, to study this research, and develop solutions. No one has been able to bring workable solutions to the issue of gun control. This is a key element in my goal of making the world a better place. No matter how many people I reach and help, if the issue of violence is not solved, there will always exist a missing piece that puts poor people in danger.

"What I need the four of you to do is dig into the information that exists in the form of studies and conclusions reached. The way you will accomplish this is to do your homework. Assimilate all the information that has been brought forward by all the parties in this debate.

"Make use of all current and emerging technologies and rely on your intuition. I believe in you, and I confer upon you the gift of wisdom along with eidetic memories to better deal with complexities that have foiled attempts to come to grips with random violence. Find a place for your base of operations, get settled, and I will meet with you in a month."

Joshua placed his hands on each of their heads and they were changed, ready to solve the issue of bringing violence into the light; they found that the primary components of violence in the world were mass shootings, gun control, mental health, police violence, and poverty. After the meeting, the four friends immediately began doing research into every piece of information ever published.

The four left the parking lot, proceeded to Logan Airport, and bought airline tickets to Washington, D.C., where they took a cab to their destination, the Library of Congress, their new base of operation.

After they reserved a conference room large enough to install four workstations and a meeting area, each of them pored through all the information about the occurrence of mass violence over the past five years. After days of reading and assimilating newspaper articles, periodicals, and the Library of Congress records of congressional dealing over the past five years, they met to compare notes.

The conclusions they reached were very similar:

1. Gun violence accounted for many of the incidents involving multiple victims.
2. No single area of the country stood out as a hotspot.
3. Mental health was a key factor in most violent instances.
4. Gun violence, in many instances, occurred where violence was not a part of the fabric of the community.
5. There was evidence that violence was linked to a person's genetic makeup.

They needed a strategy.

They discussed areas of concentration not analyzed before. Lisa recalled part of Joshua's direction, "Utilize current and emerging technology." She outlined several possibilities.

CHAPTER 8

First, on her list was Artificial Intelligence (AI). This is a branch of information technology that maximizes the assets found in relational databases and advanced querying to simulate human thought and replicate physical properties. Robotics is a primary beneficiary of AI.

Next, there was genetics and DNA modeling. This area of science enables scientists to predict a subject's characteristics and alter traits that may define aberrations in a person's DNA coding.

Finally, there was Plato, a massive AI application created to assist in problem-solving and gaming. Due to the vast, fast hardware and software available to businesses large and small, to governments and to scientists working on everything from healthcare to astrophysics to chess, issues in today's world are resolved quickly and accurately using Plato. While Plato works on a project, it learns, so that future iterations of the project will be more accurate.

Mike, Joe, and Larry sat and listened. When Lisa was done, they began their feedback.

"Let's narrow the focus and begin with a single area that might prove fruitful," Larry said.

Mike, Joe, and Lisa agreed.

"In my reading, I found that quite a lot of genetic research is going on. Neuroscientists have conducted studies of genetic aberrations related to violence. This may be a good point to start our research," said Joe.

After much discussion, they agreed that they would visit Plato headquarters. Much data would come directly from this phase of the project.

Plato resided in the "cloud" on a massive network. There is no known limitation to its capability and capacity. If a capacity problem occurs in a Plato project, new cloud storage is added dynamically.

When the four friends arrived at the Plato site, they were granted access to every part of the facility. They had already uploaded the data to be analyzed. Plato was queried using Artificial Intelligence to develop and manipulate the thousands of studies, which the team of four had introduced. Over the next thirty days, Plato churned the information and reported what it had found in each iteration, using the previous round as a baseline.

After only five hours of processing, Plato sent this message to the four friends:

"I have arrived at an approach."

The team of four gathered around the workstation where the encouraging message appeared. They entered their security protocols, and Plato approved their security packages. After this housekeeping was finished, they began to query Plato about specifics.

Here's what Plato revealed:

1. Violence has been linked to genetics.
2. There are specific genetic areas related to violence.
3. The specific genes where potential changes are needed.

(Individual genetic data was masked so that a hacker would not cause a breach in Plato's impregnable network.)

The conclusions from Plato yielded a roadmap through the genetics of violence. There was no one specific solution. The

CHAPTER 8

best use of Plato was to identify triggers and circumstances that result in violent outcomes and to construct an AI roadmap on how to build a solution that, over time, will result in lessening the rate of violence in the U.S.

After fifteen days, Joshua showed up to check whether reaction to their "solution" would be positive. However, he was compelled to express to them the need for a single specific conclusion. What is the gene that directly relates to violence?

They responded by assuring Joshua that they would remain in Washington to guide the project until Plato defined specific strategies to identify areas where genetics could be used to define high probability of individual matches. This was the strategy. It would take a few weeks for Plato to choose individuals who had a proclivity for violence. After all, Plato was looking at a pool of possibilities that could then be matched with violent tendencies and access to guns.

Although it sounded like a daunting and impossible project, the advantage Plato gave to this team in terms of AI and decision-making that other contemporary teams could not reach would prove to be the Rosetta Stone in this massive endeavor. Joshua had made the right decisions by empowering his four confidants.

The wars in the Mideast had begun again. Oil fields were targeted and destroyed. People in the region were uprooted from their homes, and they moved into overpopulated refugee camps. There were upwards of three million people in these hellish places.

The success of the airline industry in the USA was a thing of the past. Fatal crashes and their inability to respond to market demands coupled with the inexpensive cost of living in South and Central America caused very high unemployment in the airline industry in the United States. Especially vulnerable were the states of Washington and California. Because of the USA's dominance in the airline industry, most states were affected. Fewer people were traveling, especially by airplane. The USA was on the brink of economic collapse.

On the other hand, Germany was experiencing economic growth and was the leader of the European nations who once were a part of the European Union. They were also building their military might again. There was a resurgence of Nazism and White Supremacy, putting the world on notice that the old Germany would rise again. Their automobiles were second-to-none in the world, including the conglomerate formed by all the Japanese manufacturers. It was the largest corporation in the history of the world. Their engineering expertise in the manufacturing areas were typically German, simple, and elegant. Their economy was growing.

This was the world in the 2020s and 2030s. Joshua knew from the beginning what his destiny was.

Wherever the world was changing, people lost their jobs, had their savings disappear, or lost themselves in despair and hopelessness. The net result was that more and more people were put on the street. Homeless people were present in every major city on the globe. They lived by day panhandling, and at night, they slept anyplace they could find.

Homeless cities sprang up in old tunnels, in abandoned properties, in subways, on sidewalks, and in city parks. The average person in the 2040's was appalled by these people, but there were only a few who chose to try to help them. In 2040's, there was an aversion to religion. Joshua was looking forward to his new challenge.

CHAPTER 8

Joshua boarded a plane to New York City; he intended to become one of the 200,000 homeless in the USA. He dressed in the garb of a poor person so he would blend in with the homeless. He deplaned at La Guardia airport. He spent his last twenty dollars on a taxi ride to the Bronx. From there, he took a subway to 42nd Street. He found Bryant Park crammed with homeless people. It was about 9 p.m. He found a patch of grass along a fence. He checked his backpack for a blanket. He laid down and pulled the blanket over himself. He fell into a deep sleep. At dawn, he was awakened by two homeless men in an argument over an old newspaper. He arose and folded his blanket into his backpack. He looked around and saw that the park was full of homeless men, women, and children. He stood in their midst and beckoned them closer. He began to speak to the crowd. He asked them to pray with him, and they did. He spoke about despair and depression, and he told them he came to help poor people. He also spoke of hope.

Joshua heard them talking about him and asked the crowd, "Who do you think I am?"

They looked at each other puzzled. "Just who is this gentle person?"

At this point, a police car pulled up and two police officers got out. They approached Joshua with their batons in hand. Joshua reached out and touched the two officers. They looked at him, surprised. As they gazed into his eyes, they realized Joshua was a special person, to whom they should not bring any trouble. They nodded and walked back to their car. From that point in time on, the park had police protection 24/7.

Joshua began speaking to the crowd again. He explained that he came to help all people out of the darkness and into the light. He spoke of a forgiving God who loved all of them. Then, he ceased his speaking and raised his arms to heaven and spoke words that no one understood. There was a roar of thunder and a bolt of bright light. At this point, he lowered his arms. He invited anyone who wanted to speak with him to come forward. Several of the homeless came forward and spoke with Joshua with respect and love. They realized immediately that this was a special person who could help with their problems. He spoke to about a thousand people a day. He influenced all of those to whom he spoke, convincing them to overcome their despair with the hope of rewards in heaven.

When he was finished, he slowly walked to a nearby street vendor whom he had befriended. The vendor gave him a warm pretzel and a bottle of water. Joshua thanked him and found an inconspicuous place to eat his daily bread.

This same scene was repeated day after day for five years. He was recognized as a messenger sent from heaven. The prophet of Bryant Park was gaining recognition and renown, which he knew he needed to avoid. He preached and the crowd listened to the promise of a better life on Earth and in heaven.

The Sacra Sindone heard the reports of the prophet who was preaching and healing souls in New York City. They dispatched three contract bullies to apprehend and bring this young man to the Vatican for questioning.

One evening, while he was eating, Joshua had a vision of the three thugs making their way to Bryant Park. He knew his best strategy was to blend in with the homeless until the danger passed. He walked a short distance to the entrance to Bryant Park.

One of the officers on the police detail recognized the danger in these three strangers. The officers located Joshua and put him in the police car. They waited until the three henchmen left,

CHAPTER 8

then drove Joshua to the bus station on 42nd Street. They bought him a ticket to Chicago, saw to it he got to the bus, and the bus rolled away. Joshua had escaped from the Sacra Sindone. He had existed in this world of the homeless for three years.

CHAPTER 9

Sacra Sindone
The Vatican

Sacra Sindone is a Catholic society run by the Jesuits. In 1983, after the first attempts to radiocarbon date the Shroud of Turin had failed, Sacra Sindone took on its role as guardian. Their mission at the time was to control access to the Shroud by those outside the Vatican and to protect the Shroud from damage. As time went by and radiocarbon dating became acceptable as a fossil-dating methodology, the mission remained the same, but the policing of access to the Shroud of Turin and the protection of it became obsessive and, at times, harmful. The Sacra Sindone society became a police force to guard the Shroud.

The Shroud of Turin is purported to be the burial shroud of Jesus Christ. Legend has it, and Scripture attests to the fact, that on the first Easter, Jesus' burial cloth was left in the cave where Jesus was buried and from which he resurrected.

Sacra Sindone, The Shroud of Turin, also called the Holy Shroud, is a length of linen cloth bearing the negative image of a man. Some claim the image depicts Jesus of Nazareth and the fabric is the burial shroud in which he was wrapped after crucifixion. It is said that the image was created at the moment of the Resurrection.

On the first Easter Morning, some of Jesus' followers went to the tomb in which Jesus was buried. They found the rock in front of the cave was rolled away, and the tomb was empty. All that was there was the burial cloth of Jesus. What was intriguing about the Shroud was that there was an image of a crucified man on the Shroud. The disciples took the Shroud, and so started the story of the Holy Shroud.

The Shroud was taken out of the Holy Land during the Crusades. It was moved from town to town to protect it from damage or destruction. It was caught in a fire in a church in France and rescued by some monks. The fire marks remain on the Shroud. Eventually, the Shroud ended up at the Vatican. It was determined that this holy relic should reside at the Cathedral of Saint John the Baptist in Turin. It remained in Turin for centuries. In the 1970s and 1980s, people became interested in the Shroud. There were several attempts to radiocarbon-date the Shroud to prove its authenticity.

Some historians attribute the failed tests to intervention by the secret society, Sacra Sindone. Of late, there has not been any further testing of the Shroud; however, the Church considers it a sacred relic, and keeps it locked in the Cathedral of St. John the Baptist in Turin. There is only one individual who can call for testing again. The Pope is that person.

CHAPTER 10

Chicago

Before Joshua boarded the bus to Chicago, one of the police officers handed Joshua an envelope with $300 in it. He said to Joshua, "You'll need this to get you started in Chicago."

Joshua politely took the envelope. Before he boarded the bus, he stuffed it in a police department jacket in the back seat of the police car. He needed to live "homeless." He got off the bus at the Chicago 95th Street bus station. Next, he proceeded to Millennium Park in the Northeast section of the Loop. His intention was to preach, teach, and heal the homeless in this bastion of homeless people. He quickly developed a following. Word spread about the homeless prophet who was holding healing services on the beach sand near Maggie Daley Park on Lake Michigan.

From the beach, one could view the city at night, a beautiful sight. The homeless slept here and were very protective of their little city. Joshua joined their hierarchy. He became more visible, and he was always available when a homeless person needed him. He was tireless, almost as if he didn't need sleep.

But as his reputation as a healer grew, so did the demand for his healing. People from as far away as St. Louis and Little Rock made their way to his beach. He touched them very gently, and their troubles, physical and psychological, were washed away. He preached a gospel of change, love, and hope. As the numbers grew, so did the possibility of Joshua being harmed or kidnapped.

Joshua set out for the Middle East. He spoke with the captain of an oil tanker and secured a cabin for the long voyage to the Middle East. He stayed in his cabin for the entire journey, coming out only to eat and walk around. He was headed for a refugee camp in Turkey, said to be one of the most densely populated of all refugee camps. The Syrian refugee camps outside of Turkey were miserable places to be human. It fit his mission perfectly. He stepped into his role and immediately drew masses of people. They were hungry, physically, and spiritually, and they accepted Joshua and his mission.

One day, a group of brutes from Sacra Sindone showed up at the refugee camp Joshua was working in. He did not run or hide. They captured him. In a matter of minutes, he was put on a helicopter and taken directly to their headquarters in Vatican City. He was placed in isolation in a below-ground room that looked like a dungeon.

CHAPTER 11

Joshua is captured

Sacra Sindone vowed to eradicate all the people involved in The Cloning. They found the cloning lab in Arce and destroyed it. They intended to murder any of the scientists they found; only two were still alive. They escaped. They couldn't find Cindy. She had left in search of Joshua.

They found Dr. Benson and tortured him until he gave up the location of Joshua who had been kidnapped by the Sacra Sindone at a refugee camp in Turkey and placed in detention in Vatican City.

Dr. Benson escaped and sought out Pope Paul VII, who had aged quite nicely. They reviewed the life of Joshua. They formulated an answer to the question, "Did we clone Jesus?"

The answer was there all the while. Jesus is the Son of God, conceived by the Holy Spirit and born of a virgin. Cloning from the blood on the Shroud is a human exploit. But did Joshua clone as a human only? Joshua is a copy of the person wrapped in the Shroud. Did His divine nature clone? These questions and many more will be debated by theologians through the ages, and a determination will be made based on the evidence. This is just how Jesus' humanity/divinity was defined in the early Church.

CHAPTER 12

But the story isn't over. Sacra Sindone was still a nuisance and needed to be dealt with. Joshua needed freedom to follow his work on Earth.

Bill Benson was summoned to the place where Joshua was being detained. He called Cindy and arranged to pick her up at home and fly to the Vatican.

They talked about the happenings over the past three decades. They especially spoke about Joshua and his mission. They vowed to change people's lives by following Joshua. Could they make a difference? They didn't know for sure but pledged to try their best.

Joshua asked Bill Benson who his torturers were. Benson told him about the Sacra Sindone. Joshua wanted to meet with them. Benson was asked to set up the meeting, which he did. Sacra Sindone showed up at the interrogation site.

Joshua got to his feet. There was a roar of thunder and a light so bright it stunned the people in the room. Joshua began to speak. His words were heard in each person's tongue. He was bathed in a bright white light.

"I am here to change the world. My Father sent me. We in this room need to accept the change. I am in each of your lives and have been since The Cloning. With my coming, I bring a new age of peace among all of mankind. When you leave this place, accept the peace I offer. Your free will needs to guide you.

I will be there every step of the way. My work will reach thousands of poor people. We need to change the world, and you need to do your part to change people around you.

Joshua stepped down and blessed the people around the table. The meeting ended, and the people around the table filed out of the room. The looks on their faces and the way they walked told the people watching them that they had changed.

Joshua returned to Seattle to continue his life's work with homeless people. Bill Benson and Cindy went back to Boston and resumed their lives and look for a way to aid in world change. The Sacra Sindone went back to their base of operation. The Pope retired to Lake Cuomo to rest, relax, and pray.

PART 2
WHO DO YOU THINK I AM?

CHAPTER 13

November 13, 2050
Chicago

Joshua returned to Chicago's Millennium Park. He settled into a spot in the center of the homeless population, and began to preach, teach, and heal. While his message was clear and his teaching was accepted, what distinguished him from preachers and teachers in 2050 came down to his healings as more and more pilgrims visited Millennium Park.

His message was "Go out from here and change the world." His teaching was based on doing good for others. When he finished, all understood what he said in their own tongues. It is not known how many followers he acquired through his work at Millennium Park, though one can assume he had a discipleship numbering in the thousands.

However, his activity was especially noticed by an audience of people linked together by social media. The people of 2050 were technologically savvy, and their lives were on display because of social media. One new technology during this decade featured the use of holographic images with whom one communicated about topics significant to them. Holographs were 3-D images of those involved in the discussion.

At the end of his session, a young man in horn-rimmed glasses approached Joshua.

"Mr. Joshua, may I speak with you?"

"It's Joshua, and, of course, you can. What can I do for you?"

The young man told Joshua his life story in five minutes. He then went on to say that he'd communicated with holographs. Joshua needed some clarification.

"What does 'communicate with holographs' mean?"

"Well, you see, you run this app on your tablet. It calls up your friend; now you are both holographs. My friend sees me as a 3-D image, and I see him the same way.

"Can you show me? By the way, what's your name?"

"My name is Peter. I'm thirteen years old, and I go to the middle school right across the street." He pointed over Joshua's shoulder. He pulled a tablet out of his backpack and began typing on it. In a flash, a holograph of his friend appeared in their midst.

Joshua was astonished. He began talking to the holograph.

"So, what does one talk to a holograph about?"

The holograph responded, "How about you?"

"What is your name, Mr. Holograph?"

"My name is Luke"

"Okay, what do you want to know about me?"

"Well, people are saying you are a messenger from God. Are you?" Luke asked.

"Yes, I am sent from God."

"Peter, did you hear that? He is sent from God."

"My parents were right. They say you are a holy man sent to us to teach and heal sick people," said Peter.

"And Luke, who do you think I am?" Joshua's eyes were blue as the ocean as he stared into Luke's holograph eyes.

"I say you are God."

CHAPTER 13

Joshua began his mission in the streets and in homeless camps. He targeted the most needy and desperate souls. He went directly to them. He started in common areas where homeless people lived.

Joshua's mission took him wherever the growing homeless populations existed. He had no permanent address. He relied on good people to recognize his humanitarian acts and to support his activity. He gained the respect of social workers and first responders. He also guided those who were close to him to focus on his mission.

He never coerced his followers, but rather urged them to develop those programs which benefited the lonely and desperate in our society. He accepted no money or valuables. He owed no one but his believers, whom he rewarded with satisfaction and pride in their good deeds. He didn't use technology, but he was well-versed in where misery existed. His followers came from very diverse backgrounds, ages, and educational levels. As his band of followers grew, his goal of changing the world became more attainable.

Everyone whose life he affected was changed. Their problems began to go away. They realized that they couldn't refuse his help because of his goodness. And once they agreed to follow Joshua, they developed a sense of hope. His following grew every day. His purpose was well-defined; his followers were happy and committed.

Joshua was on his way to change a world in need of change.

CHAPTER 14

November 24, 2050
Thanksgiving

Bill Benson and Cindy were preparing Thanksgiving dinner for two, if you can imagine that. All the same recipes, as if it were for ten people. There would be lots of leftovers for the weekend.

"What do you think Joshua wants us to do to help him change the world? I've been thinking that he had a plan to accomplish changing the world. He has done it before. He heals people. How do *we* change the world?" asked Bill.

"He chose us as two of his disciples. He must know we can help him. I am having the same thoughts as you have. But we need to think of our Joshua and the way he works. I was thinking about our role; here's what I think," said Cindy. "I think we should ask him. Get a feel for what he thinks. Maybe offer to help him with his mission."

"Okay. Let's plan on going to Chicago for Christmas. We'll buy him dinner and discuss his plans. That's a great idea. I'm glad I thought of it."

They sat down to eat, rejoicing in their good life together. They were especially happy to have been the parents of Joshua.

Bill and Cindy Benson called Joshua the day after Thanksgiving. They told him they wanted to see him and talk to him about his mission and how they could help. Joshua agreed to go to dinner, very low-key, he stressed, to help them.

So, on December 2, Bill and Cindy boarded a plane bound for Chicago. They chose a morning flight landing at O'Hare at 11:00 a.m. They arranged a late lunch at a local neighborhood restaurant. They waited at the bar for Joshua to arrive. He came in wearing jeans and a hoodie. They hugged and joked for a minute or two. Then they sat and ordered their lunch. While they waited, Bill asked Joshua what he had in mind for his and Cindy's help to change the world.

"What I was thinking is that you two are such likable people. I thought you might get involved in a social issue that affects young people and their families like drug addiction and opioid misuse. It seems like a natural fit. I am concentrating on the homeless and their issues, physical, and psychological. The three thugs who captured me have devised a way to use their former purpose of protection of the Shroud to bring believers and skeptics to Turin to pray and be healed. I will be there three times a month to help with healing, but the Shroud is the center of spontaneous acceptance. The visitors will not be allowed to touch the Shroud. That would put too much stress on the ancient burial cloth. They would be thrilled just to view the Shroud and the image of the person who died covered by it."

"We can and will get involved with a social issue that is visible to the public. You know we are not afraid to take on a challenge like the drug and opioid crisis," said Bill Benson. "What do you think, Cindy?"

Cindy looked into Joshua's eyes. She had tears building in hers. "I think we can do what you are suggesting. I'm very proud of you and your accomplishments. It's not every woman who has a son who is going to save the world."

CHAPTER 15

November 24, 2050
Headquarters of Sacra Sindone

The three members of Sacra Sindone whom Joshua had commissioned to help him change the world had reported back to the head of the Society on what happened at the meeting with Joshua, his parents, and Pope Paul VII. They were castigated and grounded by the Society. The Society hierarchy deliberated their fate as the three waited. Their names were Pietro, Santino, and Domenico. None of the three volunteered commentary on the mission Joshua gave to them. They knew they needed to discuss it but were afraid to bring it up. Finally, Domenico spoke.

"He wasn't just a man; Joshua is sent from God. We need to accept that and decide how we do what he asked."

Santino spoke next. "I agree, and the sooner we tell them, the better."

Pietro, "But what do we tell them?"

Santino volunteered, "Let me handle that."

They went on talking for two hours. Then the meeting to decide their fate at Sacra Sindone broke up. The Society leader approached them with his head down.

"You failed in your mission to apprehend Joshua. We need to capture him. He is a threat to the Shroud. As fate would have it, he is back in Chicago drawing attention to his actions. There is an opportunity to get him there."

"Sir," said Santino, "we were just discussing what we should do to help Joshua change the world. We believe he is sent from God. He cures the sick, and it is said he casts out demons. Unless he so chose, we probably would not have even been able to apprehend him. We have decided to help him in his mission to change the world. Can't you see he is the clone from the Shroud? He isn't a threat to us. His coming validates that the Shroud is, in fact, the burial linen of Jesus Christ. We should make this known. We should let the world know that Joshua has come to save the world. We should let all people around the world know that The Cloning was successful. The Shroud has not been compromised. It is time we do our best to help Joshua change the world. The Shroud should be displayed regularly. It should be treated just as we treat the Blessed Sacrament. The position that we must take regarding the Shroud is that it brought Jesus back to us to make the world a better place for mankind. You must see this."

"What are you asking us to do? Are you suggesting that our community must change what we have been doing for eight decades?"

"Yes, sir, we are."

The leader of Sacra Sindone left the three. He decided to nap to refresh himself for an afternoon meeting of the Society. It didn't take long for him to enter a deep sleep.

He dreamed that Joshua was in the room.

Joshua spoke, "You are the key person in Sacra Sindone. As such, I need you. Your three members, who learned of my mission, know what it is and agreed to support it. I'm here to change the world to do good deeds. I expect nothing in return.

CHAPTER 15

"Your mission is to protect the Shroud at all costs. I am asking you to take on a different role. I need your society to change into a visible entity which oversees showing the Shroud publicly, protecting it, and ensuring its physical integrity. You need to show people what the Shroud is and educate those who come to see the Shroud. I will help you with the role change. You need to see your world in a different way. You need to come out of the shadows. I'll show you what needs to be done and support you along the way. Take my plan back to your comrades. Emphasize that by agreeing to my request, your society gains papal recognition and support. Your members gain recognition as supporters of Sacra Sindone, a Roman Catholic relic. The veil of fear and intimidation will be lifted."

The leader awoke from his deep sleep. He had a strange, peaceful feeling after his siesta. He was anxious to share their new direction with the members. He summoned the resident members to a meeting to divulge the new direction for Sacra Sindone.

So, what followed was a retelling to the Sacra Sindone of the three members' suggestions to him. The Society accepted the suggestions and began preparing for the presentation of the Shroud in Turin.

The Society leader went on the Italian *Today* show to tell the world what Sacra Sindone is and the fact that three of its members had reported about Joshua. He said Sacra Sindone's purpose took on a whole new meaning after The Cloning. He explained what The Cloning was. Then, he took questions by means of computer conferencing. His announcement marked the first time The Cloning was mentioned publicly. People were anxious to see the Shroud and the clone it produced. There was excitement in this airing of Joshua's mission on Earth. Will this embellish Joshua's work, or will it backfire to jeopardize his mission to change the world?

"We've protected the Holy Shroud for a long time. It's time to treat it as a holy relic with respect. So, we have decided to make the Shroud the focus of adoration in Turin. There will be daily benediction and adorations for pilgrims from all over the world. We feel this is a logical extension of our original purpose: to protect the Holy Shroud from those who are not directly involved with it."

He paused to take questions. Joshua watched from a restaurant.

CHAPTER 16

Pope Paul VII

Pope Paul VII lived a very nice life, serene and holy. He was contemplative, and his life was filled with peace and prayer. He had taken on full papal responsibilities, but he was getting bored. He kept in touch with the Bensons, and he needed a dose of Bill Benson to lift his spirits.

He moved into his suite at the Vatican. He was pacing back and forth like a lion at dinner time. Finally, he settled down, dialed Bill Benson's cell phone, and waited.

"Bill Benson here. What can I do for you?"

"Hello, Dr. Benson. It is good to hear your voice. How have you been, and how is Cindy?"

"We are doing well. We just got back from seeing Joshua in Chicago. He's fine and enthusiastic about the six of us joining in his mission. We asked him what he was thinking of our role. We needed some guidance, plus we really wanted to see him."

"You know, Bill, I have been wracking my brain about what my vocation should be in this historic movement. And I'm drawing a blank. In fact, that's why I called you."

"Have you thought about the Church taking the leadership role in this? I don't mean in the traditional way. I mean you should influence the cardinals toward real change, based on

Joshua's message. He wants to change the world, and Jesus built the Church. However, few families are active in the Church."

"That's a lot to ask of this ancient institution, but you are right. The Church must lead in affecting change in the world. It can't just be a willing participant. It must show the way and direct the changes that will come."

CHAPTER 17

Seattle
Joshua Moves On

The plans to "Change the World" were made. Each of the disciples had a role. It was time to put the plan into motion.

Joshua completed his mission in Chicago. He spent five years preaching and teaching in the loop. He reached almost a million people, and he'd done so in a way that was patient and kind. His cloning and coming were well known by now, and there was an openness to accept him as sent from God. At first, there was skepticism, but as the years went by and Joshua's healing power was felt almost every day, skeptics fell away and Joshua was accepted with little question.

He packed up one night, bought a bus ticket to Seattle, Washington, and boarded the bus at 1:00 p.m. the next day. In the early 21st century, this trip took fifty-four hours. In 2045, due to new technology, buses ran safely about 100 mph, taking a little over twenty hours.

Joshua's flock in Seattle were uprooted technical people, the ones who lost their jobs due to cutbacks in the airline industry. He contacted a former homeless person a week prior who helped bring together over 100 placement professionals to set up some inspirational sessions. It seemed that Joshua's good work had made him a sought-after motivational speaker. The placement professionals promoted the seminars, and Joshua spoke to the displaced techies about dealing with loss and the effect of the job losses on their families. He spoke about hope and joy during radical change. He told them they had the power to change the world. He also healed those who needed healing. He spent eighteen-hour days working toward saving the world. As one athlete who had experienced his healing power stated, "He's the real deal, man."

His first seminar was held the next Monday at noon. It was attended by over 1,000 people. Joshua began to speak, and the group quieted. They listened to his message about saving the world, overcoming despair, and sharing his values with others, especially with family. Then, he opened the meeting up to questions.

"Joshua," said the first man, "who are you, and why are you here?"

This question did not surprise Joshua. He knew it would come, just not so early. He stared into the man's eyes, and gave him this answer:

"I come from God. I am here to tell you all that the world needs to change and that it is within your power. I am here in Seattle to help ease the pain of change to a section of the people who worked in Seattle, then lost their livelihoods. Before you can help change the world, you need to accept that you have the power to change the world. I am here to bring that message from the Father and to ease your troubles."

He reached out to the man. The man flinched ever so slightly, and Joshua immediately stepped away. "May I bless you and take away your pain?" The man nodded slowly and approached Joshua. Joshua put his hands on the man's head.

CHAPTER 17

He sensed extreme anxiety. Joshua prayed in a language no one recognized. The man turned to him and hugged him.

"I believe you; I believe," the man said.

CHAPTER 18

Dorchester High School
Brookline, Massachusetts

Bill and Cindy got home from Chicago and began working out their mission. They began speaking to each other as if they knew what was in each other's mind. They would need to contact hospitals to gain their involvement in opioid use. They also needed to speak with traditional drug companies and outpatient rehabilitation professionals. Their plan was to form a series of non-political task forces with no ties to lobbyists, or ties to either house of Congress, or to any other branch of the federal government. The idea was that the further this entity was from donations, lobbyists, or government, the more likely that it would be a major part of the healing process.

Then they spoke about drug addiction. They pulled up statistics on Google. They went online to study the effect of opioids and other drugs on families. They learned from their research that in urban areas, the overwhelming percentage of the population that died from overdoses were minorities.

They decided to take a break from researching and do some field trips into Boston's inner city. They spoke with families, clergy, police, and healthcare providers. They were faced with a sorrowful story of death by suicide of the drug victims, but when their families got involved in changing the environment surrounding these deaths, there was progress on a wider scale. The involvement of loved ones hurt by a drug-related death was a key ingredient in solving the problem of the overuse of drugs.

They turned in that evening knowing what they would do to help change the world. They would get started the very next day.

Their day started at 6 a.m. They began by contacting Dorchester High School. They spoke with the principal, a woman in her early fifties. Her name was Mrs. Adele Dobson. They introduced themselves as Joshua's parents. She had heard of Joshua, the young man with a special gift of making people feel like he was talking directly to them when he spoke.

The Bensons told Adele about The Cloning. They told her about Joshua's mission to change the world. They spoke of the day Joshua had a meeting, which included Pope Paul VII and three members of a secret society called Sacra Sindone, which protects the Shroud, and the Bensons. Each person at the meeting was asked to "go from this place and help me save the world."

As far as the Bensons knew, each of the people at the meeting had developed a way to help Joshua save the world. "That is precisely why we are here." They spoke of their part in the mission, to solve the problem of drug addiction in teenagers. They spoke of their research and the conclusions they drew from it.

"We believe that a key piece of this plague on our society is the unbearable grief that drug addiction at all ages leaves with their families. We believe that if we can develop a network of families who are willing to go out into the community and share their experiences which led up to the drug addiction, we would begin by identifying people who had overdosed and died. We would bring the parents of those victims to the table to compare their experiences. The meetings would be hosted by

CHAPTER 18

professional moderators. There would be caseworkers, psychologists, nurses, and doctors on hand to break logjams and share experiences. There would be a sense of accomplishment along the way, but the real nugget will be a set of solutions that work. We will invite Joshua to speak about hope in the face of despair. We believe that bringing these people real hope in a future they helped to shape will go a long way to changing the world."

They paused and asked Adele if she would help by supplying a list of Dorchester teenagers who had lost their lives by overdosing, suicide, or any other drug-related reason.

Adele reacted to this plan in a very predictable way.

"I love that you asked for my help, but I need to consult with the lawyers and the school district. There are a lot of issues that touch on privacy and security, and many of these people live below the poverty level. I've been through this type of for-the-good-of-humanity projects. I'm not sure Dorchester can be involved."

Bill Benson felt a bolt of lightning hit his abdomen. He knew there would be pushback because of budget restraints or legal issues, but he didn't expect it on the first interview. They said their goodbyes and left. There was no conversation in the car all the way home.

As they drove to the front of their house, Bill Benson said, "So, we can't use Dorchester as our initial project. Let's do some homework to find a few other candidates."

They made a list of the most recent suicides by overdose in Boston. They delved into each suicide. Who, where, when? Soon, they had a picture of the neighborhoods with the most tragedies. They looked at each other and realized that the statistics they were looking at described real people, real sorrow.

They spoke for a while and concluded that their initial approach would not work.

"If we asked Joshua what he would do, what would he do?" The light went on, and they knew what they had to do.

"He would seek out the families of the victims. He would speak with compassion to each of the families about their sorrow and despair. He would listen intently, making eye contact often. He would never set up a bureaucracy of committees and meetings, which would lead families further into hopelessness. He would seek to abate their sorrow. He would seek remedies to help them. He would try to ease their pain."

"Once they hear the message of hope and salvation, they will possibly be open to speak about their tragedies. And the bottom line is not how many we speak to, but how many we reach." They realized that each time they could pull someone from the brink, they would help save the world.

They called each of the families affected and explained their mission. They talked of Joshua, The Cloning, and the direction Joshua had set to save the world. The response was pretty good, but they knew that these people were dealing with grief so with each step they took, they had to keep that in mind.

So, they went out to the neighborhoods in Boston to help Joshua save the world.

CHAPTER 19

Torino, Italy

There were 100,000 pilgrims in Torino, Italy on a bright, sunny day in May of 2050, and it was only Monday. They were lined up for at least two miles, but they didn't mind. The Shroud was outside the cathedral on display, and each of the pilgrims needed the healing power of the Shroud. This was the Shroud of Turin being guarded by the Sacra Sindone.

Torino latched onto the importance of the Shroud. Pietro, Santino, and Domenico were promoted to the position of guides of the Shroud. From guards to guides. Nice! But there was always the chance of an unknown threat of damage aimed at the Shroud or the pilgrims. So, they remained on alert all the time they were working.

They were put center-stage in the display of the Sacred Shroud. They knew about its history and about The Cloning. They were asked by Joshua to "go out from here and help me change the world." They understood the importance of the Shroud as a means of saving the world.

Suddenly, the crowd felt the ground rumble, and then the sun appeared to grow two times larger. There was a feeling of joy in Torino this day. Santino broke the silence that had overcome the pilgrims. "It's Joshua. Joshua is in Torino." They looked across the plaza, and they saw him. As usual, he tried to shun the attention; he stopped in the middle of the plaza, borrowed a microphone from a band that was practicing there, and he began to speak. In a moment, he had the crowd's full attention. He spoke of his mission to save the world. He acknowledged the hopelessness and despair in the world, which he said he would help with, and he implored the pilgrims to help him save the world. He then made an offer to the assemblage.

"I will be in the cathedral waiting for prayers and a benediction. There will be hymns and blessings."

Then, Pope Paul VII arose and began his introduction with this, "My dear friends, I have convened this session to discuss and explain a rather radical departure from Church rubrics. Rather than bringing attention to that which doesn't matter, I'd like to introduce Joshua of God."

Then Joshua came forward and placed himself in the middle of the College of Cardinals.

"I am Joshua of God. I was cloned from the blood shed on the Shroud of Turin, the burial cloth of Jesus of Nazareth. In my human body, as a child, I received a message from my Father in heaven. He told me to save the world. He gave me the gift of healing. I was raised by Bill and Cindy Benson. At eighteen years old, I set out to complete my mission.

"I have worked with the homeless in New York, Chicago, and Seattle. As I preached and taught about hope in the face of despair, I gained followers. Many of those who are part of my discipleship were elevated through healing. There was an uprising in the Vatican, and I eventually won my detractors over. During the uprising, I managed to bring together six individuals to assist in my mission. At this point, each of them has begun his own mission for saving the world.

CHAPTER 19

"We are now at the point where the world needs to hear the good news. And you have a major role in that. We believe the Church should take the leadership role in spreading the news of my coming. You must act in a special way to make it clear that the Church is changing, and you must be the example to all those who are acting to support my mission. You need to create a new spirit of ecumenism and reach out to all your Christian brothers and sisters. I never knew nor did I ask the religion of my followers. I did repeatedly ask them, "Who do you think I am?" Religion is a human construct that has caused much pain and anguish among the people of the world. It needs to be stripped away, and a new world order formed of all people, no matter what they call our Father.

"We need to bring those of you who need me. Please take care in moving to the church. Be mindful of your brothers and sisters who also want to speak with me."

A line formed into the church. It parted as Joshua approached. He asked them to respect the House of God, and the crowd complied. Then, Joshua began to heal the people in the front row. He worked his way from front to back. Then, he allowed the next group to fill the church. He went about his healing with pauses only for a drink of water. He went on, hour after hour, in one-on-one sessions.

When night fell, he left it up to each pilgrim to continue or stop. He administered his healing powers until the early morning. He was just as vital and energetic at 3 a.m. as when he started. But the Sacra Sindone stepped in because people in line were nodding off. So, Joshua stopped for a few hours and rested. There were at least seven days of healing ahead of him.

He rose at 6 a.m. and began again where he had left off. Again, he worked at healing both physical and psychological problems. And again, those he healed had experienced a joy they spoke about. "Joshua is sent from God. He cured my blindness and made me see again," said one who was healed. And each one who was healed pledged to help Joshua "save the world."

Joshua spent seven days healing. Then, as quickly as he showed up on Monday, he packed up and left. He went back to Seattle and resumed his mission there.

CHAPTER 20

The Vatican

Pope Paul VII called for a meeting of the College of Cardinals. He set the date for June 15, 2050. His only agenda item was Joshua. He took the suggestion Bill Benson had given him, "Put Joshua in front of the cardinals." The purpose of the meeting was to convince the cardinals that the Church should take the lead in supporting Joshua in his mission to save the world.

The Pope made plans for Joshua to be picked up at his session. He sent three Swiss Guards to bring Joshua to the Vatican. There were no incidents. Joshua arrived at the Vatican on June 15. He met with the Pope, who explained the purpose of the meeting with the cardinals. He told him he believed the Church should take a leadership role in Joshua's mission of saving the world. He told him he should treat the cardinals as he treated all his followers.

"Tell them who you are, where you come from, and your mission."

"Bill Benson told me what to expect. Let's do this together." said Pope Paul.

"Bring all my followers together so that I can speak to them all at once. I expect the number of followers to be about three million. As we go forward, that number will get larger, and their influence will spread rapidly.

"Pope Paul VII and I spoke about an encyclical, which would announce a Church council to explain my coming to the world. That is a way to meet with my followers while demonstrating that the Church has the good of all who follow the Father in mind. My followers and yours must be one single body. We need to combine the two factions so that the Church and my discipleship are one. I will return to my Father's house soon. My mission will be complete by the time I leave."

The Cardinals spoke to each other in small groups. They whispered so that Joshua and Pope Paul VII wouldn't hear their deliberations. It looked as if the cardinals were enthusiastic about Joshua and his origin and mission.

After a few minutes, Pope Paul called for order. He began to speak.

"So, the story has been told. May I ask my fellow bishops what you have to say about Joshua and his mission?"

There was a pause in the chatter. The cardinal from Portugal spoke first.

"What you are saying is that the Church needs to change radically the way we minister to our flock. You are saying our flock is all of mankind and all that we have developed since Jesus left us needs to be altered and reconstructed. I am personally apprehensive that this mission is far too vast for our followers to take on. Is there another way?"

Then, the cardinal from Brazil got to his feet and spoke in a low and mellow voice. "My dear brothers in Christ, please listen to me. I have a confession to make. I refer to the passages in Scripture that reference the second coming quite often. It is very important that a member of the hierarchy of the Catholic

CHAPTER 20

Church be aware of the theology behind the second coming. To be honest, I am confused about what Jesus promised us about His second coming, and I know that I am in the dark about how to recognize the sacred event. Therefore, I am open to what Joshua claims. What if what Joshua has said is true? Then ignoring it and denigrating his claim of who he is would be comparable to the Sanhedrin mocking Jesus."

Another cardinal from Canada began to speak. "I, too, can't say I would recognize the Savior if he appeared in our midst. I believe the authentication of the claims that arise from a holy man, who came to us as the Savior, will take a long time as it did in the early days of the Church. In the meantime, we need to pray, so that we arrive at a conclusion based on our mutual faith. Besides, I have a strong sense that Joshua will go about the mission he has been given by his Father with or without our help. Therefore, I suggest we take a vote to see where we all stand on the proposition Joshua has made to us. A simple 'yes' or 'no' to the question of 'should we take a leadership role in supporting the Joshua mission, based on our faith in him."

Joshua knew what the vote would be before it was taken. Of the thirty-two cardinals present, eighteen voted "yes" and fourteen voted "no."

Pope Paul thanked the cardinals and informed them that they would all be asked to take part in the gathering of Joshua followers. He asked for their help in selecting a proper venue Where would they ever find a venue to accommodate three million or more followers?

The answer to that conundrum came almost immediately the next day. Six of the cardinals did their homework.

In fact, no single venue existed on the planet. The largest of the stadiums in the world is in Pyongyang, North Korea. The top ten range from 120,000 seats down to 100,000. There were land areas that could be transformed into amphitheaters, but the number of people a natural amphitheater could accommodate is far less than three million. Furthermore, the size of such a land modification would prohibit interchange among the followers. It would approach approximately five miles long and three miles wide. The word "unmanageable" applied very nicely to such an undertaking.

However, technology in data communications had progressed over the last two decades, which made it possible to tie together millions of people over communications networks using fiber optics, satellites, and faster, smaller personal computing technologies using Artificial Intelligence. Most of the cardinals knew of these advancements through communications with their flocks.

Here's what they came up with:

- Choose one large venue where Joshua would speak to his followers.
- Use current technology to broadcast the message Joshua will give to the world.
- Choose the venue based on weather and security.
- Make it a live event to capture the mood and the true meaning for his followers and the rest of the world.

They spoke to Joshua and Pope Paul about the plan. After much discussion, they all agreed to move forward. So began 2051, Joshua's most important year on Earth.

CHAPTER 21

The Coming Event

Despite the cool reception at the Vatican on June 15, all the cardinals were delighted to be involved in planning and implementing the enormous gathering of Joshua's followers. They helped in wording the announcements of the event to comply with Church protocols. They suggested venues in their home countries. They hired experts in communications to develop the network to touch the ends of the earth.

It would take one year to plan and implement all the pieces of the event. When one thinks about this undertaking, one is reminded that cynics might say, "If Joshua is from God, why doesn't he just make the event happen?"

And therein lay a peek into his divinity. He must have had a reason for all the anomalies in this story. For that, one needed to assume he was fully aware that those who were helping him had free will. For his followers to grasp his full meaning, his true place in the physical, metaphysical, and theological universe and for their experience to be enduring, they had to see that they had helped Joshua change the world.

SUMMER OF 2051

The cardinals met in endless sessions, trying to select the main venue where Joshua would deliver his message to the world. The Pope suggested that the Vatican should be where Joshua would broadcast his message. In the past, many enormous pilgrimages would end in St. Peter's Square, Vatican City. All major Church announcements were made by the Vatican, and with a little ingenuity and a lot of work, the cardinals would make this happen.

And so, the work began. The Pope and the cardinals were actively engaged in various phases of development. However, they needed to see to it that pre-Joshua Church commitments were not ignored. They would work together to see to it that all Church business was conducted properly during Joshua support days.

CHAPTER 22

November 24, 2051

The day finally arrived. And the date selected for Joshua's day was six months ahead of schedule. The encyclical was sent three months prior.

The day of Joshua's address to the world had been set for Friday, November 24, 2051. It would take place in the Piazza San Pietro, St. Peter's Square. There were stadium-size TVs all over Vatican City and Rome. Crowds formed in Vatican City during the early morning hours. Joshua began speaking at 9 a.m. He spoke from the Pope's balcony above the Square.

The security was unprecedented. The Vatican Police, the Swiss Guard, the Rome Police, Interpol, and heavy security presence from the USA were there and very visible. The Vatican was ready for the biggest event in its history. There was a feeling of joy and peace among believers and non-believers. The entrances to St. Peter's Square were blocked by police until about 8:30 a.m. This was done to give access to the front of the Square to as many as possible. Of course, the Pope and his cardinals would occupy reserved seats in the front of the Square. A papal procession would lead the people into the Square.

8 A.M.

There was a rustle of activity at the entrances to the Piazza. The Pope and his entourage formed a procession and began entering the Square. They proceeded to the section set aside for the Pope and sat down. The Pope remained standing with his two arms raised. When he waved, the floodgates burst, and people floated in. The security people kept the crowd flowing and directed them to the open seats. When the seats ran out, the crowd was directed to open areas where they could stand. It took an hour to get the crowd settled down. Similar gatherings were formed in neighborhoods of Rome that could hold many people. This did not happen by chance. It was part of the planned logistics. The cardinals did a great job. In each neighborhood, there was a fountain, plaza or some central space where stadium TVs were installed on all the buildings surrounding the central point.

AT PRECISELY 9:15 P.M.

Joshua appeared on the papal balcony overlooking St. Peter's Square. The applause that greeted him escalated as people realized he was there. They knew this was a special occasion. It was loud and joyous, and it lasted for about ten minutes until Joshua quieted the crowd. Then, he began to speak with no microphone and all who were watching Joshua heard him loud and clear in their own tongues.

"I am Joshua of God. I was sent by the Father to change the world. I was cloned from the blood shed by Jesus on the Sacred Shroud. The Shroud will never produce another like me. When I was very young, the Father sent me a message in a dream. He said, 'I tell you go forth and save the world.' He gave me the gift of healing to help me with my mission. I will be leaving soon, so I need your help. I need you all to go from here and change the world. That is, give people hope in the face of despair. Be kind and help one another."

He raised his arms, and there was a rumble that sounded and felt like an earthquake. The crowd blurted a loud "Oh!" and then there was a cacophony of murmurs. Joshua settled the crowd and began to speak again.

"I am with you, and I have been there for all of you since The Cloning. In a little while, I will leave and return to the Father. My mission is complete. I have begun changing the world based on my own relationships with the people who came to me. Many of them are here today. I have also put in place the means for my followers to complete the mission. Help them. Do what they ask, for it is I who is exhorting them. I leave you the gift of understanding and fortitude.

"Use your gifts wisely. Bring nothing into suspicion. Act in a way the Father taught Jesus. Do good for others. This is important because it will come from the goodness that resides in us."

Then, he paused. There wasn't a sound. Then a light shone from him that was bright as the sun. In an instant, he was gone.

The people present that evening were changed. They went from that place to save the world.